Poppy's Pancake Day

A humorous rhyming story

First published in 2006 by
Franklin Watts
338 Euston Road
London
NW1 3BH

Franklin Watts Australia
Hachette Children's Books
Level 17/207 Kent Street
Sydney
NSW 2000

Text © Sue Graves 2006
Illustration © Jane Eccles 2006

A CIP catalogue record for this book is available
from the British Library.

ISBN 0 7496 6551 3 (hbk)
ISBN 0 7496 6558 0 (pbk)

Series Editor: Jackie Hamley
Series Advisors: Dr Barrie Wade, Dr Hilary Minns
Design: Peter Scoulding

Printed in China

For my beautiful granddaughter, Isabelle – S.G.

READING CORNER

Poppy's Pancake Day

Written by
Sue Graves

Illustrated by
Jane Eccles

W

FRANKLIN WATTS
LONDON•SYDNEY

Sue Graves
"My family loves pancakes, but no one is very good at tossing them. Have you ever made pancakes?"

Jane Eccles
"I'm pretty good at making pancakes – I'm not as messy as Poppy anyway! I especially love drawing animals."

Mum was feeling poorly.

She felt faint and very ill.

"I think I'll go to bed," she said.

"I must have caught a chill."

Poppy made her cups of tea.

Dad bought a magazine.

But Mum just sat there sneezing,
and looking rather green.

"Poor Mum could do with cheering up," Dad said. "She looks so pasty.

"Why don't we try to make her smile by cooking something tasty?"

9

Poppy looked at recipes to
see what she could find.

There were lots of pies and pastries,

and cakes of every kind.

"Oh dear!" said Dad. "Those look too hard. Let's make something easy.

What about a sandwich ...

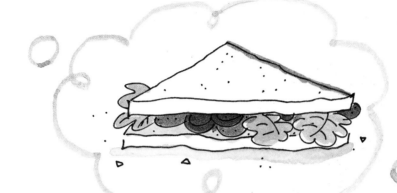

... or toast that's thick and cheesy?"

"Pancakes are her favourite food,"
said Poppy with a smile.

"We could make lots of different ones
and stack them in a pile."

So Dad got eggs and butter;

Poppy flour and jam.

Then she got out the weighing scales while Dad looked for the pan.

Poppy whisked the mixture.

She turned the mixer high.

The pancake mix spun round so fast
it hit Dad in the eye!

Soon the mix was ready.

"Time to cook them now," Dad said.

"Mum is going to love them.
She can eat them up in bed."

Dad poured the mixture in the pan,
then tossed it in the air.

The pancake landed with a plop ...

... on top of Poppy's hair!

"My turn now," said Poppy.

She gave the pan a flip.

The pancake shot up skywards,
and then began to tip ...

... It hovered for a moment ...

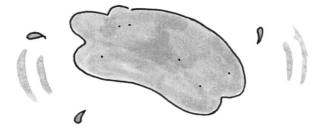

... and then spun round and round.

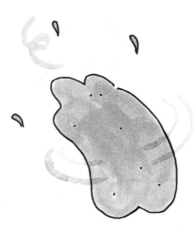

And with a very squelchy splat,
it landed on the ground.

So Dad and Poppy mopped the floor
and cleaned up all the mess.

Then went to see how Mum felt,
now that she had had a rest.

"I'm feeling better now," said Mum.

"Why look, it's half past three."

"Let's go and make some pancakes as a special treat for tea!"

Notes for parents and teachers

READING CORNER has been structured to provide maximum support for new readers. The stories may be used by adults for sharing with young children. Primarily, however, the stories are designed for newly independent readers, whether they are reading these books in bed at night, or in the reading corner at school or in the library.

Starting to read alone can be a daunting prospect. READING CORNER helps by providing visual support and repeating words and phrases, while making reading enjoyable. These books will develop confidence in the new reader, and encourage a love of reading that will last a lifetime!

If you are reading this book with a child, here are a few tips:

1. Make reading fun! Choose a time to read when you and the child are relaxed and have time to share the story.

2. Encourage children to reread the story, and to retell the story in their own words, using the illustrations to remind them what has happened.

3. Give praise! Remember that small mistakes need not always be corrected.

READING CORNER covers three grades of early reading ability, with three levels at each grade. Each level has a certain number of words per story, indicated by the number of bars on the spine of the book, to allow you to choose the right book for a young reader:

GRADE 1	GRADE 2	GRADE 3
50 words	130 words	250 words
70 words	160 words	350 words
100 words	200 words	450 words